BABY ALIENS GOT MY TEACHER!

KT-432-848

PAMELA BUTCHART

nosy crow

Look out for:

THE SPY WHO LOVED SCHOOL DINNERS

MY HEADTEACHER IS A VAMPIRE RAT!

ATTACK OF THE DEMON DINNER LADIES

TO WEE OR NOT TO WEE!

THERE'S A WEREWOLF IN MY TENT!

First published in the UK in 2014 by Nosy Crow Ltd
The Crow's Nest, 14 Baden Place, Crosby Row
London, SE1 1YW, UK

Nosy Crow and associated logos are trademarks and/or registered
trademarks of Nosy Crow Ltd

A CIP catalogue record for this book will be available from the British Library.

Printed and bound in the UK by Clays Ltd, St. Ives Plc

Papers used by Nosy Crow are made from wood grown in
sustainable forests.

ISBN: 978 0 85763 237 1

www.nosycrow.com

Contents

I Am NOT Making This UP!

You know how sometimes you try to tell your mum and dad something REALLY important and they say stuff like, "Ah-ha, that's good," or "Go tell your dad," or "Don't be silly," or "Can't you see I'm on the toilet?!"

1

Like the time I found a crisp shaped EXACTLY like Mrs Cunningham who lives upstairs and when I showed Mum she just said, "No thanks, you eat it." I obviously did NOT eat it. I put it in an envelope and carefully posted it through Mrs Cunningham's letter box. Because that's what I would want someone to do if they found a crisp shaped exactly like me (also called a crisp twin).

Anyway, one time me and my friend Zach who lives downstairs ran home from school to tell Mum something EXTREMELY IMPORTANT about an INCIDENT that had happened that day. But she didn't listen.

Even though we were all sweaty and red and out of breath from running. And Zach had fallen and cut his knee and everything! But Mum just gave me a LOOK like I was making it up and said, "Don't be silly, Izzy," just like she ALWAYS DOES! Mum always thinks I'm making stuff up. She says I have a

WILD IMAGINATION.

And I say that I can't help it that weird stuff always happens to me!

So I told Zach to tell her, because she NEVER shouts at Zach or tells him HE'S

making things up. One time, I asked Mum why she shouted at me and not at Zach when we coloured in Dad's head when he was sleeping. And she said, "I'm not Zach's mum, but I am YOUR mum, so I'm ALLOWED to shout at you!"

So Zach told her about the INCIDENT at school, and guess what? Mum phoned his mum and she came up and SHE shouted at him. Right there in our living room in front of me and Mum and Dad and everything. I was worried she was going to start shouting at me too. But then I remembered the Shouting Rule.

I felt bad for Zach. His mum shouted REALLY LOUD and got a lot angrier than my mum did. When they left, Mum said it was because Zach's mum and dad have split up and that this was the last thing Zach's mum needed as she already had "TOO MUCH ON HER PLATE!" I didn't know what that meant. But then I remembered that, last week at school dinners, Mrs Kidd (the school force-you-to-eat-every-scrap dinner monitor) wouldn't let me leave the table until I finished EVERYTHING on my plate. And I felt sick because the stupid dinner lady had given me five ice-cream scoops of shepherd's pie. They use the ice-cream scoop for all the food at our school. Zach says that they don't even wash it before they serve the ice-cream and he knows that for a fact because his mum used to be our

old dinner lady. Anyway, I HATE shepherd's pie so I couldn't finish it all and I got really angry because I wasn't allowed to leave the table and I DEFINITELY had too much on

my plate!

So, anyway, Mum told me to go to my room and do my homework. But I said I couldn't until she listened to what had happened at school that day. But then her eye started to get all twitchy and that's what happens before she gets really annoyed and starts shouting things like, "That's it! I've had it! No holiday!" So I just left it and said sorry because I really, really want to go to Disneyland in the school holidays as we didn't get to go on holiday last summer because Dad had to work.

So I went upstairs, but I didn't go to my room. I sneaked along the hall into Mum and Dad's room and phoned Zach on his new mobile phone.

Dad says that it's RIDICULOUS that Zach has a mobile phone at his age, especially one that's better than his. Mum says that Zach's dad buys him lots of expensive things because he's not around as much as he was. I know Zach misses his dad but we don't really talk about it because Zach doesn't like to.

So anyway, I phoned Zach from Mum's room. And someone answered. But it wasn't Zach! It was somebody else! And then I remembered that we had left our school bags in school because we had run away after the INCIDENT. The INCIDENT that Mum didn't want to hear about. So I slammed down the phone and dialled 999. Because that's what the police officer that came to our school said to do in an EMERGENCY.

And this was an

EMERGENCY!

The "I-Had-an-Accident" Clothes

Even though the INCIDENT happened on Friday, I'm going to start this story from Monday, because lots of other stuff happened before the INCIDENT.

Jodi (our friend and third witness) says that we have to call what happened an

INCIDENT and not an ACCIDENT because an ACCIDENT is when something happens by accident and an INCIDENT is something that happens that is not an accident. And what happened at school on Friday was definitely NOT an accident.

On Monday, me and Zach walked to school like we always do, because our school is right beside where we live. And Jodi's mum drove Jodi right into the playground even though Mr Murphy (the Head Teacher) shouts "NO CARS ALLOWED!" out of his window EVERY morning.

I don't think Jodi's mum even hears Mr

Murphy shouting because she has her music up really loud and I can usually hear what song she's singing along to even though all the windows are rolled up.

Jodi says her mum is practising for X Factor because she's bored of working in the bakery and that she's **"SICK TO THE BACK TEETH"** of smelling like sausage rolls. But Jodi says her mum's not very good at singing and that one time the woman who lives upstairs came down to their door and shouted at her mum and called her a **"NIGHTMARE NEIGHBOUR!"** and said it sounded like a cat was being strangled.

So that's when we started to spy on the woman who lives upstairs because as Jodi said, "How does SHE know what it sounds like when you strangle a cat?" And this was a very good question. I have two cats and Zach has one, so we followed her for a while to make sure she wasn't a Cat Strangler. But she didn't really go anywhere and then one day she caught us peeking through her letter box and she phoned the police and even

though we told them about her being a Cat Strangler we still got into big trouble. But I didn't really mind because now she knows that **"WE'RE ON TO HER!"** and Zach said that she was **"UNLIKELY TO STRIKE AGAIN"** with us watching her. So our cats are safe.

Anyway, I also once heard Mr Murphy tell the office ladies that Jodi's mum was a **"NIGHTMARE PARENT"**. And I didn't think that was a very nice thing for the Head Teacher to say. So I told Jodi and she told her mum and now every time Mr Murphy goes into the bakery, Jodi's mum gives him the cakes that have fallen on the ground.

But I'm secretly glad that Jodi's mum can't sing very well because that means she still has to work in the bakery. So when we go to Jodi's house there are always loads of doughnuts and yum yums and Bakewell tarts because her mum gets to bring them home for free. I've not decided what I'm going to be when I grow up yet, but I'm thinking about becoming a baker.

So anyway, me and Zach were walking up to the school gates when Miss Jones (our horrible teacher) drove past really fast and splattered us with a massive puddle. I

screamed, but Zach screamed even louder because he was standing nearest to the road and he got completely SOAKED! Zach screamed even louder than the time I put a pea in each finger of his gloves. Zach is TERRIFIED of peas. His mum says he has a PHOBIA about them, which I think means he's scared he's going to turn into one, but I'm not sure.

Anyway, I got really wet too

and the mud splattered all over my new bag. And Zach got mud all over his teeth because he had his mouth open when Miss Jones splashed us. So we had to go to the school nurse because we were soaking wet and she made us wear the spare "I-had-an-accident" clothes and sent us to class.

At least we **BOTH** had to wear the "I-had-an-accident" clothes. Because if it had been just one of us, everyone would have thought we had had a **REAL ACCIDENT**, like Maisie Miller had last year when Jodi made her laugh too much.

When we got to class, Miss Jones didn't

17

even ask us why we were late. I thought that was really WEIRD because usually Miss Jones asks you for a note and if you don't have one she tells you off and makes you go back down to the school office to get one.

I don't understand why she makes us do that because it takes two and a half minutes to get back down to the school office, then another three minutes to wait for the office ladies to stop ignoring you and open the glass window, then another two and a half minutes to get back upstairs to the class again. That's a total of eight minutes. So if you're only two minutes late in the first place,

you end up being ten minutes late!

So me and Zach just went and sat down in our seats and told Jodi why we were wearing the "I-had-an-accident" clothes. Then Jodi told us that Miss Jones was being really nice today and that she said we didn't have to do our maths work this morning.

I was really happy that we didn't have to do our maths because even though I am quite good at maths, I hate doing it because it's boring and I have to share a book with Gary Petrie. And he always picks his nose and puts it in between the pages and calls it "A CRUSTY SURPRISE".

But I DID think it was really weird that Miss Jones didn't want to do maths that day because everyone knows that Miss Jones LOVES maths. She loves it so much that one time when nobody got the answers right in the maths quiz, Miss Jones got really annoyed and shouted at Jodi, and Jodi got upset and shouted, "Miss Jones, if you love maths so much why don't you just marry it?!" And then she got kept in at break "for cheek" and got double maths homework.

So anyway, we decorated our exercise books instead and that was better than maths. But I was a bit suspicious about why

Miss Jones was being so NICE because she's NEVER nice. Zach said maybe it was because she felt bad for splashing us. But I said that Miss Jones hadn't even noticed that she'd splashed us because she was driving like a MANIAC.

I used to think our old teacher, Miss Riley, hated us. One time I wrote MISS RILEY IS MEAN on the board when she wasn't looking. But then when she saw It she started crying and I felt really bad. That's when I found out she probably didn't hate us because if you hate someone I don't think you really care if they call you mean.

But I had been sure that Miss Jones actually DID hate us because she ALWAYS moaned at us (even when we weren't doing anything wrong). And she NEVER gave us free time or treats like the other nicer teachers in the school gave their classes.

One time Maisie Miller was swinging on her chair and she fell off and hurt her arm and I SWEAR Miss Jones had a tiny smile on her face.

But the time I found out that Miss

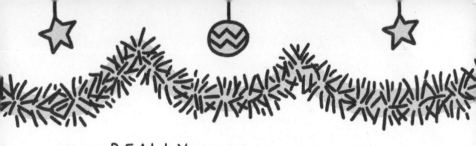

Jones REALLY hated us was when Jodi
had one of her JODI TANTRUMS (also
called a JT) in the middle of the Christmas
Concert because Gary Petrie
was supposed to be a
lamb but he kept saying,
"MOO! MOO!" every
time it was Jodi's turn
to speak. And Miss Jones
didn't do ANYTHING
about it.

So Jodi started kicking
everything and pulling her hair out (just like
she always does when she has a JT). Then she

shouted, "YOU HATE ME, MISS JONES, DON'T YOU?!" and Miss Jones didn't even deny it! So then Jodi kicked the manger and the baby Jesus fell out on to the stage and everyone in the crowd gasped and someone said, "OUTRAGEOUS!" and Jodi started crying.

I don't know why everyone got so upset because it wasn't like it was a REAL baby that fell out of the manger. Our baby Jesus is made of plastic.

At lunchtime, Miss Jones let us out five minutes early because she was going OUT

for lunch. I thought that was also weird because Miss Jones NEVER goes OUT for lunch. She usually just sits at her desk and eats a smelly Cup a Soup. Then when we come back into class we try to guess what kind she had that day by smelling the air.

Last week I guessed MIN-E-STRO-NE and when Zach checked in the bin to see the wrapper he couldn't believe that I'd got it right. But that's because I saw it in her drawer earlier when I was looking for the Big Stapler. But I didn't tell him that.

So anyway, on Monday everyone thought Miss Jones was great because we didn't

have to do our maths and also because we got one hour and five minutes for lunch. Then after lunch she didn't get back until two minutes after the end-of-lunch bell had gone.

I wanted to ask her if SHE had a note, but Zach said, "No, don't! We've got to keep her in a good mood so she says we don't have to do any work again!" And guess what? That's EXACTLY what she said!

Teddies and Diseases

On Tuesday, Miss Jones was wearing make-up. I'd never seen her wearing make-up before. Zach said it made her look like she was one of the young teachers, but I thought she still looked like she was about thirty or something old like that.

I was just about to sit down at the table when I saw the weirdest thing ever. There was a teddy bear on Miss Jones's desk!

YOU'RE GREAT!

You might think that's not very strange at all, but Miss Jones isn't really a teddy bear kind of person. She's more of a hates-puppies-and-thinks-kittens-are-ugly kind of person.

The teddy was pink and had "You're Great!" written on its tummy and a rose in its paw. Everyone STARED at it but nobody knew what to do so we just sat down. And then Miss Jones said, "Let's all make Valentine cards today!" and gave us all pieces of pink card with little red love hearts and put *The Greatest Love Songs Ever 6* on the CD player. I thought this was weird for three reasons:

Reason 1 – Miss Jones was smiling (a lot).

Reason 2 – Miss Jones was singing.

Reason 3 – It was October.

Everyone just stared at each other. I think

we were in shock. Like the time me and Mum were waiting for the bus outside the library and I leaned against the glass in the bus shelter. But I didn't know that the glass had been taken out because of VANDALISM and I fell backwards.

I almost rolled on to the road and got hit by a bus, but a man who was there dropped his peanuts and grabbed me before I did. Afterwards, Mum kept saying, "THANK YOU! THANK YOU!" and trying to give the man money to buy new peanuts but he wouldn't take it. And then on the bus I didn't say anything at all. And I still had my apple in

my hand and I had squeezed it so hard that my nails were stuck in it and Mum said that I was in shock.

Anyway, Zach likes making cards so he said he was going to make one for his mum to cheer her up and I just said OK and didn't make fun of him like I sometimes do.

So me and Jodi sat together and tried to find out why Miss Jones was being so weird. Jodi said that one time her aunty started doing lots of weird things, like saying, "Good morning, Jeffrey!" to an orange and pouring milk on her violin. The doctor had said that it was STRESS and sent her aunty to bed for

a little rest.

Then I remembered that at Cousin Clare's wedding, Mum had acted really weird too. She had kept telling everyone that she loved them and had thrown her shoes out of the window.

Dad said that Mum had **"BEEN A BIT TIPSY"** that night.

So me and Jodi pretended to make Valentine cards, but really we made a list of

all the things that might be wrong with Miss
Jones.

DISEASES
MISS JONES
MIGHT HAVE
Stress
Tipsy Disease

But then we couldn't think of any more
diseases Miss Jones might have, so we
showed it to Zach and he said that writing
a list was a stupid thing to do. He said that
he liked Miss Jones now because she was

being nice, and told us to stop doing the list.

So we fell out with him until the bell went. Then when we were putting our coats on, Jodi said that her mum would give me a lift home if Zach didn't say sorry for saying the list was stupid and that he'd have to walk home on his own. So Zach said sorry and Jodi said, "Apology accepted!" and we walked home.

Miss Jones IS a Weirdo!

On Wednesday, Miss Jones stood at the door and patted our heads when we walked into the classroom. Then she started calling us all weird names like "pumpkin" and "peach" and "pomegranate" when she was doing the register. I thought maybe we were going to be starting a new project on fruit or something. But we didn't. Instead, Miss Jones gave us all sweets and said we could watch a film!

I got really excited because Miss Jones **NEVER** gives us sweets or lets us watch films. Not even when it's the last day of term. So we all got comfy on the floor with the big cushions. And then Miss Jones sat on the floor with us! I'd never seen a teacher do that before.

The film was OK to begin with. It was about a huge meteorite that was heading towards Earth and everyone was panicking because

the Earth was going to explode. But then it got all soppy and Miss Jones cried so much that Zach nearly had to get the nurse just to calm her down! Then Miss Jones just sat there hugging her teddy and saying, "THIS IS MY FAVOURITE FILM OF ALL TIME."

That's when I knew Miss Jones had gone BONKERS. If this was her favourite film, why would she be crying so much all the way through it?

That afternoon Miss Jones said that it was high time we did some MEDITATION.

So we sat with our legs crossed and said, **"UMMMM UMMMM UMMMM UMMMM,"** for ages.

I didn't really understand what MEDITATION was for but Miss Jones said it was for RELAXING and she must have been right because Maisie Miller got so relaxed that she fell asleep on my leg. Or maybe she just fainted again. You can never tell with Maisie Miller.

One time I tried to show Maisie my ingrown toenail just before I had my TOENAIL REMOVAL OPERATION. But she fainted before I even got my sock off.

We were supposed to keep our eyes closed during the meditation, but I peeked to see if anyone else was peeking and

Zach was peeking too. And then he saw me peeking and whispered, "Look! Look at Miss Jones!" So I did. And she had her eyes closed and she was waving her teddy slowly backwards and forwards in the air and chanting, "AAAAAAA-UUUUU-EEEEEEE-OOOOOOOOO."

When we were finished meditating, Zach said that Miss Jones really WAS being weird and asked to see the list again. He said he didn't think that Miss Jones had tipsy disease or stress. But he said that she might have CRAZINESS. So we added it to the list.

Then Zach said he remembered watching

a film with his mum one time. He said that in the film there was this ALIEN who wriggled inside a woman's ear and took control of her body. He said that the alien woman had acted really nice to everyone and then when they became her friends she had put little baby aliens in their ears and THEY became aliens too! He said that nobody ever suspected she was going to do something bad to them because she was so nice to everyone, but really she was planning an ALIEN INVASION. So we added BABY ALIEN IN THE EAR to the list.

But then Maisie Miller woke up and heard

what we were talking about, and Maisie Miller gets REALLY scared at stuff like that. Before we could stop her, she'd started crying and Miss Jones had seen her and come rushing over.

I thought Miss Jones was going to start shouting and asking us what we had done to make Maisie cry. But she didn't. She just gave Maisie a big hug and said, "Now now, my little lamb! What's wrong?" and that just made Maisie even MORE scared and she started screaming.

In the end, Maisie Miller's mum had to come and collect her because the school nurse said that she was "HYSTERICAL".

Time
Bomb
Teddy

Nothing could have prepared us for what happened on Thursday. Miss Jones was absent. And Miss Jones is NEVER absent.

I was late for school that day because I got locked in the bathroom AGAIN. And Dad had to take the door off its hinges AGAIN to get me out. Then Dad took me to school and said not to tell Mum what had happened because she would get angry with him for still not fixing the bathroom door.

When I got to school, I went straight to class and didn't bother going to the office for a note because Miss Jones didn't seem to be asking for notes any more. But when I got to class I saw that Mrs Seith (the Deputy Head Teacher) was sitting at Miss Jones's desk! Mrs Seith told me to go to the office and get a note "AT ONCE!" So I ran down the stairs to the office as fast as I could because the Deputy Head is SERIOUSLY SCARY.

I heard that one time she made every single pupil in the school cry during an assembly just by making her eyes go really wide.

Then when I was being ignored at the reception, I heard the office ladies talking about Miss Jones's teddy. They said that the Head Teacher's ears must be BURNING. And then they said, "This TEDDY SITUATION is a TIME BOMB waiting to

EXPLODE!"

At lunchtime me and Zach and Jodi ate our lunch and then sneaked off to The Den to talk about what I'd heard the office ladies say. We have to be really quiet when we're hiding in The Den because it's under the stairs that everyone walks up to get to the toilet. One time the caretaker found us in there and we thought we were going to get into big trouble.

But then he said we could stay there if we wanted and gave us the key. He said it was OK because he was retiring next week and he didn't care what the Head Teacher thought anyway. He said that if HE was a pupil at this school HE'D need somewhere to hide every now and then too.

So now there's a new caretaker, but he doesn't even know about the little room under the stairs. And even if he does find out, we're the only ones with a key.

The Den is the best. There's lots of great stuff in it like a sink and a kettle and a toaster. Zach makes us all cups of tea when we have

secret meetings. But we just hold them and don't drink them because we don't have any milk or sugar and we're not allowed to boil kettles so it's cold tea anyway. Jodi keeps saying that she's going to bring three slices of bread from her house so we can have toast. But she keeps forgetting.

So anyway, Zach got the tea ready and Jodi took out the list of DISEASES MISS JONES MIGHT HAVE and told me to tell her EVERYTHING I'd heard the office ladies say. So I told them how I'd heard the office ladies say that the Head Teacher's ears were BURNING and that Miss Jones's teddy was actually a TIME BOMB and that it was going to EXPLODE! And then Jodi said, "I think I know what's wrong with Miss Jones." But then someone knocked on the door and Zach screamed!

Then we heard a voice say, "It's me." But we didn't know who ME was, so we didn't move. But then the voice said, "It's Maisie. Let me in, quick!"

I couldn't believe it! Nobody was supposed

to know about The Den
except for us and the
old caretaker! Jodi
rolled her eyes and
gave Zach a LOOK.
But he got annoyed
and said, "What? It
wasn't me. It must have

been Izzy!" And then I got annoyed and said
that it wasn't me either. So I opened the door
and pulled Maisie in before anyone saw her.

Maisie told us that she'd known about The
Den for AGES because she saw us sneaking
in one time. Maisie's a scaredy-cat, but she's

all right, and she's really small so we said that she could join the secret meetings in The Den as long as she didn't tell anyone.

But then Jodi said, "There's some SERIOUSLY SCARY STUFF we need to talk about, Maisie!" And I thought Maisie was going to start crying. But she didn't. So Zach made her a cup of tea. And then Jodi was just about to tell us what she thought was happening to Miss Jones when the bell rang. So Jodi said, "The secret meeting will continue at my house tonight. 6pm. Be there!"

Baby-Alien-in-the-Ear

We'd never had a secret meeting at Jodi's house before, as we usually had them in The Den. I didn't know what to bring so I just brought a bag of crisps, four biscuits from the cupboard, my good pens and Dad's torch.

Jodi lives just a few houses down from us, so me and Zach walked over. When we got there, Maisie Miller was waiting outside Jodi's flat with her mum. Maisie was wearing a long, padded coat and gloves and earmuffs, even though it wasn't that cold and Zach only had a T-shirt on.

Maisie's mum gave Maisie a big hug and then she said, "Look after my little angel! I couldn't bear it if anything were to happen to her!" So we said we would. Then when we got up to Jodi's flat, Maisie had to wave out of the window to say she was safe before her mum got back in the car. I had to help Maisie take her coat off because she couldn't really move. Then when I got it off I saw she had **ANOTHER** coat on underneath, which I thought was weird. But Maisie **IS** a bit weird, so I didn't say anything.

Jodi's mum made us do **THE TOUR**, even though me and Zach have been to Jodi's like a million times before. But Maisie hadn't, so we all had to do **THE TOUR** again.

Maisie looked a bit confused. I don't think she's ever seen a house like Jodi's before. Jodi's mum watches those EXTREME HOME MAKE-OVER programmes where people say things like, "I think my house is boring. Can you make it more like a jungle?" And then they do. I like watching that programme too because sometimes the people who change the house get it all wrong and when the owners open their eyes they get a shock and get really angry!

Jodi's house looks like a princess's palace. Everything is pink and gold and sparkly. Jodi and her mum share a bedroom because

Jodi's mum says they are more like sisters than mother and daughter. They've even got bunk beds (which is brilliant).

I asked Mum if I could have bunk beds too but she said no. So I told her about how Jodi

had bunk beds and how she shared them with her mum. And Mum said that if I really wanted bunk beds I'd have to share a room with her. So I said I didn't want bunk beds any more because I like having my own room all to myself, and also because Mum SNORES.

Jodi and her mum have another bedroom that used to be a beauty parlour where Jodi's mum painted the neighbours' nails and waxed the hairy ladies' moustaches. But now it's a recording studio so she can practise her singing.

After THE TOUR, we gave Maisie's coats to Jodi's mum and went into the bedroom.

Jodi had already made a

STAY OUT!
SECRET MEETING!

sign before we got there so we put it up.
Then we pulled all the covers off the beds
and sat in a circle on the floor. And Jodi said,
"Are you ready?" and we said yes. And then
Jodi said the secret meeting had officially
begun. I said that I'd do the writing, because
I'm good at lists and organising. And then
Jodi said, "I think I know what's wrong with
Miss Jones." And we all went really quiet.

And then she said, "I think Miss Jones is an ALIEN. She's got a baby-alien-in-the-ear! Just like the film Zach told us about!" And I thought she was probably right, because that would explain why Miss Jones was acting nice all of a sudden.

We couldn't believe it. Our teacher was an alien! And then Zach said, "I bet she's planning an ALIEN INVASION! That's why the Head Teacher's ears are burning! She put a baby alien in to turn him into an alien and now she wants to turn us all into aliens too!" And then Maisie had to lie down for a bit.

Glow-in-the-Dark Milkshake

So we waited for Maisie to wake up. Then we went through to the living room to use Jodi's mum's computer to do research about aliens. We found lots of information and pictures of aliens. But some of the pictures were a bit scary and Maisie was starting to get a bit wobbly again so Jodi's mum said that it was time to stop using the internet and that it was time for cakes instead. So we had cakes and the really good strawberry milkshake that only Jodi's mum can make.

Maisie had never had Jodi's mum's milkshake before. At first she was scared of it because it's REALLY pink (like, glow-in-the-dark pink). But then when she tried it, she liked it and had five glasses.

Since we couldn't use the computer to research, Zach said maybe we could interview people like they do on TV. Jodi said that was a **BRILLIANT** idea. But I said that I was the one who was in charge of the research, so it was up to me what we did next. But luckily I thought doing an interview was a **BRILLIANT** idea too so that's what we did.

We interviewed Jodi's mum because she was the only one around to interview. We asked her what she could tell us about **ALIENS** and she told us to all sit down and listen.

I had to get Maisie to help me do the notes because Jodi's mum talks a lot. But this is

what we found out:

ALIENS

1. They are nice.

2. They are peaceful.

3. They come to Earth to make new friends.

4. They can read minds.

5. They are not green like everyone thinks. They are actually very pretty (and sometimes glow).

At the end of the interview we asked Jodi's mum if she had ever met an alien before. And she said, "Not yet. But I'd love to!"

So we thanked her for the interview and went back into the bedroom. We all agreed that it looked like Miss Jones really WAS an alien because she was being really nice to us all of a sudden (number 1). And not moaning at us like she usually did (number 2). She was also going OUT for lunch now instead of staying in her room with her smelly Cup a Soup on her own (so maybe that was number 3).

And then Maisie got scared that Miss

Jones was going to start doing number 5. But then I said, "Forget number five! What about number four! If Miss Jones can read our minds then SHE knows that WE know that she's an ALIEN!"

So we came up with a plan. The plan was that when Miss Jones looked at us we would all sing, "LA LA LA LA LA," really loud in our heads. So if she tried to read our minds she wouldn't be able to hear anything (except for "LA LA LA LA LA").

Then Jodi said, "What about what the office ladies said? About Miss Jones's teddy being a time bomb! What are we going to

do?" And then Zach said,

"WAIT!"

and we all jumped and Maisie did a little yelp. And he said that if the office ladies knew Miss Jones was an alien, they must be aliens too! And then Maisie got so scared she was pink-sick everywhere.

Plans, Diversions and Smelly Toes!

On Friday, me and Zach left for school extra early to make a plan to find out if the office ladies were aliens too. But when we got to The Den, Jodi was already there and she said she had **"BEEN UP ALL NIGHT"**. And then she said, "We've got twenty minutes until the first bell so LISTEN UP!"

Zach asked where Maisie was and Jodi said that her mum said that Maisie's mum was taking her to the doctor's today after all the vomit. Maisie's mum said that Maisie must have an ear infection now too because she kept screaming, "MY EARS ARE BURNING!" in the middle of the night.

So we listened to Jodi's plan and looked at all the drawings and lists she had made in her bed last night when her mum went to sleep. And then Jodi said, "Any questions?" and Zach said, "What if the office ladies catch us?" And Jodi said, "That is NOT an

option!" And we agreed.

When we got to class Miss Jones was back. And so was her teddy. I hadn't noticed it before, but the teddy looked a bit weird. It had a wonky smile and its eyes looked far too shiny.

We still didn't know what Miss Jones was going to do with her teddy, but we knew that it was definitely some sort of TIME BOMB.

YOU'RE GREAT!

Jodi stared at the teddy. Her eyes were really wide and she wasn't really blinking. She looked scared, and Jodi never gets scared about anything! Not even the time we crawled inside her gran's attic and found a huge snakeskin cocoon at the back (which meant there was a huge snake up there!). I jumped back down but Jodi stayed up there for ages with a mop saying, **"HSSSSS HSSSSS,"** to try and get the snake to come out of its hiding place. But then Jodi's gran came upstairs and said, "What on God's green Earth are you doing up there?" And so I told her about the snakeskin cocoon and

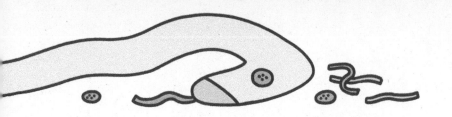

she said, "Jodi! Come down before you're eaten alive!" and then she phoned the EXTERMINATOR. Then the exterminator came in his green and red van. But after his investigation he said that it wasn't a snakeskin cocoon and that it was just one of Jodi's gran's old stockings.

Anyway, Miss Jones was being all nice again today so we waited until after break and then we started the plan.

Zach put his hand up and asked if he could go to the toilet and Miss Jones said yes and gave him a note. Then two minutes later Jodi rubbed white chalk on her face that we found in The Den from the old days. And I said, "Miss, LOOK! I think Jodi's going to be sick!" And Jodi said, "I must have what Maisie Miller has." And Miss Jones took one look at Jodi and said that I should take her to the nurse right away. So we left, and Jodi was all hunched over like she was going to be sick until we got into the corridor and then we started to run.

We met Zach at the stairs just before the school office. The plan was to get the office ladies out of the office and then search the office for ALIEN EVIDENCE. We knew that aliens would probably eat alien food, not

normal food like ham sandwiches or pizza. So if we found any alien food we'd know for sure that the office ladies were aliens too.

So Zach said we needed to create a **DIVERSION**, which meant we had to come up with an idea to get all the office ladies out of the office so we could do our search. That's when I remembered the time 6S did their cake sale in the staff room. That time I remember having to wait at the office for **AGES** until the office ladies eventually came back with all their cakes and cups of tea. So we told Zach he had to go up and knock on the glass window and say that 6S were selling

cakes again in the staff room. But he said he didn't want to because that was telling a lie. So Jodi said that telling Miss Jones he needed to go to the toilet when he didn't was a lie too. And Zach said, "That's not a *real* lie because Miss Jones isn't a person, she's an alien!" And then he said that it was OK to lie to aliens.

So I said that if the office ladies were aliens then it was OK to lie to them too. And if we found out that the office ladies weren't aliens then Jodi would get her mum to give them a big box of cakes from the bakery to say sorry for telling the lie.

So Zach said OK and walked over and knocked on the glass window and told the lady the lie about the cakes. And it worked! Loads of them came out! I never realised how many office ladies there were before. That's because you can't really see much when you're standing at the office because the glass window is a bit high and you can only really see the lady that comes to the window and sometimes you can even see all the way up her nose if she sticks her head right out.

So as soon as the office ladies were gone, we climbed through the glass window and

into the office. Jodi kept saying, "This is it. No turning back!" and I looked at her and nodded because this was SERIOUS. And then she told Zach to be the look-out but he was already looking in the filing cabinet for ALIEN EVIDENCE so I said I would be the look-out. So I sat on the chair at the glass window and made sure no one was coming and that's when I saw the name on the Sign-In Sheet.

That's the sheet at the window in the office that the office ladies make you sign if you're even ONE SECOND late for school. They even make you sign it if it's because you stopped to help a terrapin who had gone the wrong way and couldn't get back to the pond in the park. And you were just helping it not to die on the pavement. Like the time that happened to me. And then when I got my school report and Mum saw it had two **LATES** on it she said, "What is **THIS** all about, Isabella?"

So I told her about the terrapin one, but I couldn't tell her about the other one because it was Dad's fault and he had said not to tell Mum. So I said that the other one was a terrapin too and then she sent me to my room.

So, anyway, I said, "Look!" and Jodi said, **"SSSHHHHHH!"** and Zach said, "Is it them? Is it **THEM?**" and I said no and held up the Sign-In Sheet. And this is what it said:

SIGN-IN SHEET

Maisie Miller – Class 4J – 10:05 am

And then Zach said, "But we just left the classroom and she wasn't there! Why would

she sign in but not come to class?" And then I had a terrible thought. And I said, "What if the office ladies have got her?" And Jodi's eyes went even wider and Zach said we had to find her right away before they could put a baby alien in her ear.

But then we heard shoes going clip-clop in the corridor and I peeked out and saw one of the office ladies coming back. "It's too late to climb out!" said Jodi. "HIDE!" And then she hid behind the curtain. But me and Zach didn't know where to hide. And we couldn't fit behind the curtain too, so we both squashed under one of the desks.

We held our breaths when the office lady came in and shut the door. We were trapped! I was just about to whisper to Zach that we needed to create another DIVERSION but then the office lady sat down at the desk we were hiding under! We had to squash ourselves against the back as much as we could so her legs didn't touch us. Then the office lady kicked off her high heels and one of them hit Zach on the head so I quickly covered his mouth like they do on the TV to stop him from shouting, "OUCH!" and it worked.

The office lady started wriggling her toes

loads and we could hear her typing on her
keyboard. I didn't know what was going to
happen if we got caught. I thought maybe
we would get sent to the Head Teacher. But
then I remembered that the Head Teacher

was probably an alien too! So she might not send us to the Head Teacher. She might just zap us with her eye-beams or eat us or put baby aliens in our ears like what probably happened to poor Maisie.

And then Zach did a little gasp and pointed to the foot that was beside him. And I saw that the office lady had a weird squashed pinky toe, that wasn't even really a toe. It was just a stump with a tiny little nail on it that you would probably need a microscope to see properly. I wasn't sure if this was ALIEN EVIDENCE or not but it looked a bit weird anyway. The office lady kept wriggling her

toes and Zach couldn't stop staring at them.

It was starting to get really smelly under the desk and the office lady's weird pinky-stump was almost touching Zach's knee. And I needed to cough and I thought we were going to get caught, but then someone rang the bell at the reception.

The office lady stopped wriggling her toes and groaned. Then she kept typing for another two whole minutes before she finally started trying to find her shoes. So we shoved them over beside her feet so she didn't have to look under the desk and then she groaned again and got up.

We waited to hear what was happening and then a little voice said, "Come quick! Someone's locked in the girls' toilets!" And we recognised the voice . . . it was Maisie! She'd saved us!

Then the office lady said, "I can't get ONE MINUTE to myself!" and then we heard her high heels clip-clopping down the corridor. Then Maisie whispered, "HURRY! Before she gets back!" And then she said she'd meet us in The Den.

So me and Zach crawled out and so did Jodi. And then Zach saw a door and said, **"LOOK!"** and we didn't know where the door went but we could hear some of the other office ladies coming back so we just opened it and went through because anywhere was better than being back under the desk with the smelly alien toe.

But when we shut the door behind us we all went really quiet because we knew exactly where we were. We were in the Deputy Head's office!

We Should NOT Be in Here!

I couldn't believe we were in scary Mrs Seith's office. We knew where we were because last year Jodi had said that she and her mum were vegetarians now because her mum had read on the internet that all the famous people are vegetarians and it was the best thing to do if you wanted to grow your hair long and shiny.

So when we went to school dinners, the dinner lady asked Jodi what she wanted and Jodi said, "I'll have the vegetarian option, please." And the dinner lady said that the only vegetarian option was the cabbage (yuck) and Jodi said she didn't like cabbage and that she wanted a veggie burger and the dinner lady said they didn't have any of those and just put a big dollop of cabbage on Jodi's plate.

So then Jodi had a JT (Jodi Tantrum) and started screaming that it was "ALL

AGAINST HER HUMAN RIGHTS" and that she was going to get her mum up to the school. And then we made a poster about school dinners

and human rights and tried to put it up in the dinner hall.

But then we both got sent to the Deputy Head's office. So that's how we knew where we were.

But Zach didn't know where he was until I told him because Zach is usually good and doesn't get into too much trouble like we sometimes do. And when he does, he usually just starts crying and then he doesn't get into trouble any more.

So anyway, Zach started panicking because he's the most scared of Mrs Seith and he said, "Let's go before she gets back! Let's go! Let's go!" But Jodi said that we should have a quick look for evidence first since we were already in. Then she said that if the office ladies were right next door to Mrs Seith, then Mrs Seith might be an alien too!

I didn't want to stay either because Mrs Seith is scary enough just as a normal human. But there was no point in arguing with Jodi because she had THAT LOOK on her face. Like the time she decided we were going to win the three-legged race at the Fun Day and she made us practise every break and lunch for two weeks. But then Lynsey Perry said SHE was going to win with Ashley Todd, so Jodi said we had to "CRANK IT UP A NOTCH!" which meant I had to stay at her house that weekend and she made us stay tied together all weekend (except for showers and toilets). But then on the Fun

Day we won by a mile and got a trophy and everything and Lynsey Perry was furious so it was worth it.

So anyway, we started searching for ALIEN EVIDENCE. We looked in all the drawers and cabinets and then Zach said to look inside all the books on the bookshelf because he said he saw a programme once where all these old rich people kept books on bookshelves. And that some of the books weren't books at all and that they were safes and had secret compartments to keep secret stuff and jewels in. So we started looking inside all the books and then Jodi whispered, "EVIDENCE," because she found a lunch-box in Mrs Seith's bag with little fish inside it. And Zach said, "ALIEN FOOD!"

But then we heard a toilet flushing! And we looked around and saw that there were three doors in Mrs Seith's office. The one we came through when we escaped from the office ladies and two more. So I said, "She's got her own toilet!" and pointed to where the noise was coming from and then we all ran out the third door and didn't stop running until we got to The Den.

Speechless (in a Bad Way)

When we got to The Den, Maisie was already there. Zach gave her a big hug and said, "We thought they'd got you!" And I said, "Where have you been?" And then Jodi checked her ears.

Maisie told us that her mum had wanted

her to go to the doctor's because she said she was practically **"ON HER DEATH BED"**. But the receptionist at the doctor's said there were no appointments left for today, so Maisie's mum had taken her straight to the big hospital and then the doctor there said there was nothing wrong with Maisie's ears and that "Sometimes children just vomit for no apparent reason, like cats."

So Maisie's mum said, "My daughter is **NOT** a cat!" and then she asked to see another doctor. And then when another doctor came, he didn't say anything about cats, he just looked in Maisie's ears and

checked her temperature and then he said that she was fine so her mum dropped her off at school.

Then Maisie said, "I think we've got a SERIOUS problem," and then she pulled something out her school bag and said, "When I signed in the office lady gave me this because I'd been ill." And then she opened her hand and we saw it was a KIT KAT. And then Jodi said, "HARD EVIDENCE," and we knew what this meant. It meant that the office ladies really WERE aliens because they usually just ignored us.

Then Maisie's voice went really weird and

I couldn't really hear what she was saying at first because her voice was shaking so much. Like the time at assembly when I had the biggest reading to do and everyone was staring at me, and some of the older kids were laughing and my hands were sweaty and I felt sick every time I started reading and my voice went shaky because I was going to cry.

And then I heard Maisie say, "There's something else." I heard Zach do a gulp and then Maisie said, "The office lady put her hand out of the glass window and tried to touch my head. I think she was trying to put

a baby alien in my ear! So I ran!"

Then Maisie said she had been too scared to come to class in case Miss Jones was back so she hid in The Den. And then she said she had heard us when we passed to go to the office and followed us. And Jodi said, "Was there really someone locked in the toilet?" and Zach said, "No. It was a diversion, wasn't it?" And Maisie said yes and we all told Maisie she was really brave and thanked her for saving us.

Then Jodi told Maisie about being in the Deputy Head's office and the alien food we found with the little fish and then Maisie's

eyes started to do a weird cross-eyed thing
so Zach said we should all sit down and relax
and have a cup of cold tea and drink it too
this time. Because that's what
his mum and gran always do

if they've had a big fright. So we did.

After our tea, Jodi said we should go back to class ASAP so Miss Jones and the other aliens wouldn't get suspicious. She also said, "They might know we're on to them so act NORMAL." So we all said we would and then Maisie went really pale like Jodi had looked when she had the chalk-face.

Then Jodi said we should all put our hands together in a circle before we went because we were a team. Zach said we should be called

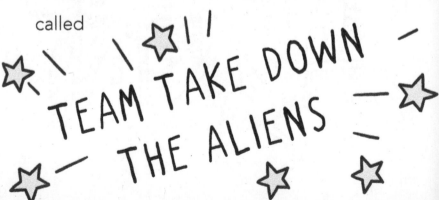

TEAM TAKE DOWN THE ALIENS

But Jodi said that was too long. So I said we could be called

ALIEN ATTACKERS

But Maisie said that sounded too scary and too violent. So we said we wouldn't have a name. But it didn't matter anyway because we didn't need a name. We had another plan.

When we got back to class, Miss Jones didn't even seem to notice how long we'd been gone. She was too busy singing and dancing with her weird, evil-looking teddy. So we just joined in and pretended like nothing had happened. I didn't know why we were dancing in the middle of the classroom.

We usually didn't do dancing unless it was country dancing with Mrs Small, who smells like corned beef. Also it was quite hard to act normal like Jodi had said we should because it wasn't exactly NORMAL to be dancing in the classroom at half-past eleven when we usually did our spelling.

I was just about to say to Zach that we should all just sit down and watch when Miss Jones started screaming and clapping her hands. And then she said, "GARY! What a beautiful dance!" And then Gary Petrie did a twirl and a jumpy thing and looked right at me and smiled really wide and said, "You look

nice today, Izzy. Would you like to dance?" and I was SPEECHLESS.

Like the time the Head Teacher said he wanted us to turn the school into a GREEN SCHOOL (which only means a school that is good at recycling and saving the planet, but me and Jodi didn't know that until after). So me and Jodi helped with the recycling and then we got green paint from Dad's shed and we painted the reception, the toilets, the steps, and two cars in the car park. And when the Head Teacher saw what we had done he was completely SPEECHLESS.

Mum said you can be speechless in a GOOD way or in a BAD way. Jodi said that she thought Mr Murphy was speechless in a GOOD WAY because we'd done such a great job, and we would definitely get the Green School Trophy from the Council now. But I think Mr Murphy was speechless in a BAD WAY because he cried a little bit.

So anyway, when Gary Petrie tried to hold my hand with his bogey fingers and get me to dance with him, I was definitely speechless in a **BAD WAY**. I looked at Jodi and she was just as shocked as I was, and her mouth was hanging wide open. Something wasn't right. Gary was dancing and being polite and Gary didn't even like dancing. Every time Mrs Small came he moaned and said that dancing was for girls and that he wasn't doing it. And then he would give Mrs Small cheek and get sent to the Deputy Head.

That's how we found out Miss Jones must have put an alien in Gary Petrie's ear.

Heads Down Thumbs Up!

We acted very normal for the rest of the day. And we made sure we didn't let ANYONE get anywhere near our ears.

Jodi said we should go everywhere together and then she said, "ACT NORMAL AND KEEP YOUR EYES WIDE OPEN

AT ALL TIMES." So we did.

Then in the afternoon, Miss Jones said we could all read our books because she was a bit sleepy from all the dancing. But I didn't read any of mine. I couldn't stop looking at the clock, because as soon as it was home time, we would start Plan 2.

Then when it was ten minutes before the bell Miss Jones said, "RIGHT! How about a quick game of HEADS DOWN THUMBS UP before the bell?" And that's when I really started to panic!

You probably know the game "Heads

Down Thumbs Up". But just in case you live in France or somewhere like that then I'll tell you what it is. Everyone puts their heads down on the desk with their eyes closed and their thumbs sticking up. Then four people are picked to stand at the front. And then when everyone has their heads down and nobody is peeking, they sneak around and pick one person each and squeeze their thumbs. Then when they have all picked someone they go back to the front of the classroom and say, "OK," and everyone brings their head back up and opens their eyes. Then the teacher says, "If your thumb was squeezed STAND

UP!" and then usually four people stand up, but sometimes there are five if someone is pretending their thumb got squeezed when it didn't. Then the people who got their thumb squeezed have to try and guess who squeezed it and if they get it right they get to swap places and be one of the Squeezers.

It's usually a really fun game, but we haven't played it for ages because Miss Jones doesn't like it. And that's one reason I started to panic when she suggested it because she doesn't even LIKE that game. But the main reason I started to panic was because if we all had our heads down and our eyes closed then Miss Jones would have FULL ACCESS to our ears because we couldn't even stick our fingers in them because we'd have to put our thumbs up.

Then Miss Jones said SHE would be one of the Squeezers and so would Gary Petrie! I didn't know what to do. I looked at Zach and he was texting on his phone under the table and I looked at it  and it said:

Then I looked at Maisie and it looked like she was already in position to play the game. But then I saw her thumbs weren't up and I knew that she had fainted. That's when I thought we were doomed.

But then I looked at Jodi and she had **THAT LOOK** in her eyes and I didn't know what she was going to do, but I knew she was going to do something. And then Jodi had the biggest JT ever!

She jumped up and her seat went flying and she started screaming, **"GO GO GO!!"** and that meant RUN, so we did. Jodi started throwing jotters and pens all over the place and then she waved a ruler at Gary Petrie when he tried to get up, and me and Zach had to carry Maisie by a leg and an arm each

but we were still going really fast because we just HAD TO, and Miss Jones was shouting,

"STOP! WHERE ARE YOU GOING?!"

and then when we were almost out the door I remembered Plan 2.

Plan 2 was that we were going to steal Miss Jones's weird teddy to find out what she was planning and stop her. So even though I was really scared and we were nearly out in the corridor, I ran back and Jodi shouted, "Izzy! NOOOOOOOOOOOO!"

Decapitation

I ran across the room so fast that I almost fell over. Miss Jones was rushing towards me and shouting, **"COME BACK!** What are you doing?!" I could tell everyone was staring at me and that they were probably all in shock, but I didn't even look. I just grabbed Miss

Jones's teddy off her desk as quickly as I could and started to run. And that's when it happened. Something inside the teddy moved! I was so shocked I almost dropped it. And then Jodi shouted,

"IZZY, RUN!"

So I ran.

We ran to the girls' toilets but Zach didn't want to come inside, he wanted to go to The Den. But The Den was too far away and we were scared we might bump into Mrs Seith who'd know we shouldn't be out of class and then we'd be in

BIG TROUBLE!

So we just grabbed Zach and dragged him into the girls' toilets and then locked ourselves in one of the cubicles.

After we all got our breath back I said, "There's something wrong with the teddy. It moved! Something inside the teddy

moved!" Then Zach got scared and said
that maybe I just imagined it like the time I

had the flu and thought his cat, Carlos, was speaking to me in Spanish. But then I said, "IT DEFINITELY MOVED!" and everyone believed me because I said it in a very serious voice and I was nearly crying because of everything.

So Jodi said we should calm down and that she would take the teddy from me very slowly and do an EXAMINATION. And then she picked the teddy up carefully and started to feel it all over its body. And then it MOVED AGAIN! And that's when Maisie shouted, "The baby aliens! THE BABY ALIENS!!"

And we all knew what she meant. Miss Jones kept the baby aliens inside her teddy! That was why she was always hugging it and stuff. Jodi went silent and was scared to move because she was still holding the teddy and then she whispered, "What if it explodes, like the office ladies said? The aliens will get out!" Then Maisie covered her ears and squealed, "Do something! QUICK!" So Zach said, "We'll bury it! Then when it explodes the aliens won't be able to land in our ears."

So Jodi said she'd be in charge of TRANSPORTING the teddy since she was good at holding it carefully. And I said we needed to find a spade

ASAP.

But then Maisie said, "Wait! I've got a better idea." And she didn't look scared any more, she looked SERIOUS and then she said, "We need to DECAPITATE the teddy!"

I didn't know what DECAPITATE meant, but then Zach said it meant Maisie wanted us to chop the teddy's head off! Maisie said the only way we could be sure that the baby aliens would be gone for good was to

flush them down the loo and see them die **"WITH OUR OWN EYES"**. Everyone agreed, especially when Maisie said it would be better than burying them in case the aliens wriggled their way up through the mud and managed to find us.

So we got ready to do the decapitation and then Jodi said, "What do you think they'll look like?" And I said that the baby aliens would probably look like little green peas with slimy arms and legs and that there would

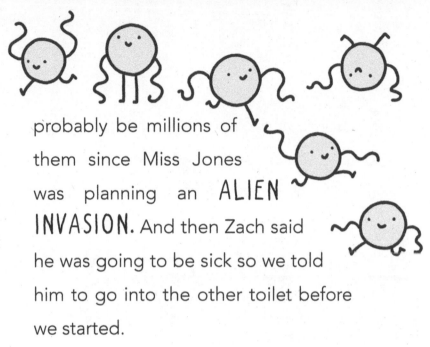

probably be millions of them since Miss Jones was planning an **ALIEN INVASION.** And then Zach said he was going to be sick so we told him to go into the other toilet before we started.

So I held the teddy and Jodi pulled its head really hard. But it wouldn't come off! So then Maisie started pulling too, but it still wouldn't come off! So I said we needed to go back to the classroom to get the Big Scissors, and then we heard a thump in the next cubicle and Zach's legs poked through into our cubical. And Jodi said, "What are you doing in there?" And then we realised Zach had fainted.

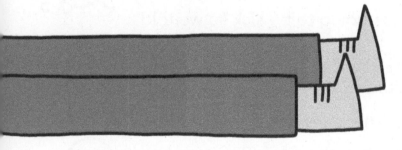

We'd never seen Zach faint before. But it was OK because Maisie said she knew exactly what to do. She gave him a drink of water from the tap and made him stay in the Recovery Position until he was feeling better.

I was surprised that Zach had fainted because usually it's Maisie who gets all scared and faints. But also because Zach said he wasn't scared of killing the aliens. And Jodi must have been thinking the same thing because then she said, "You said you weren't scared to kill the aliens?" and Zach said that he didn't faint because of the aliens. He said it was because I said the aliens were going to look like peas. And then I remembered about Zach's PEA PHOBIA. So I said that the aliens probably wouldn't look like peas and that they would probably look more like long green beans but that didn't seem to help so I just stopped saying things.

So then we stuffed the teddy behind the toilet to keep it safe and waited until two minutes after the end-of-day bell had gone and then Jodi said, "It's clear!" So we all ran along the corridor to the classroom to get the Big Scissors. And that's when we bumped right into Miss Ross who teaches 1B.

"THERE you are!" she said. "What ON EARTH do you think you're doing running out of class like that? Everyone's looking for you! Come with me." And I was just about to make up a story about why we couldn't come right now when I saw something sticking

out of her bag. I couldn't believe it. It was another TEDDY! And it was EXACTLY the same as Miss Jones's teddy!

The others saw it too and before I knew what was happening Jodi had grabbed it and shouted,

"ABORT MISSION! ABORT MISSION!"

(Which I knew meant we should forget about getting the Big Scissors and just **RUN!**) So we all ran down the corridor and Miss Ross was shouting for us to **"COME BACK THIS INSTANT!"** But we didn't.

The INCIDENT

We didn't stop running until we got all the way to the other end of the school. And then we had to stop because there was nowhere else to go. But also because Zach said he couldn't run any more because his side was hurting.

Maisie was shaking **VIOLENTLY** and she was mumbling like a weird owl, saying,  "There's two. There's two. **THERE'S TWO!**"

I couldn't believe it! There were **TWO TEDDIES!** Then Jodi said, "Someone's coming! **HIDE!**" So we ran into the staff room because that was the only place left to go. And that's when we saw the **INCIDENT**.

We froze as soon as we got in. The Head Teacher was there and so were all the office ladies. And the office ladies were all **SCREAMING** in really weird high-pitched voices and waving **EVEN MORE** teddies around! And then one of them threw a teddy **RIGHT** at the Head Teacher. And we didn't know **WHAT** was going on, but we knew that this was some sort of **ALIEN INCIDENT!**

Everyone was screaming so much that nobody had noticed us yet. But then after a few seconds everyone stopped arguing and stared RIGHT AT US. And they all looked really shocked that we had witnessed their alien fight! And that's when the scariest thing that has ever happened, happened. The Head Teacher SMILED at us. And so did all the office ladies! And then the Head Teacher said, "Erm, would you like a teddy?" And he started walking towards us with a teddy in his hand!

And that's when Jodi shouted, "DIE, ALIEN BEASTS!" and threw the teddy we'd stolen from Miss Ross right across the room and screamed,

"COVER YOUR EARS! THE TEDDIES ARE GONNA BLOW!!"

And we all screamed and ran the fastest we've ever run in our lives.

The Policeman Who Looked a Bit Like the Moon

So, like I said at the beginning of the story, when we got home Mum didn't believe us about Miss Jones being an alien, and witnessing the ALIEN INCIDENT, and almost being turned into aliens by the Head Teacher and all the office ladies, and about how Jodi had probably saved us. And neither did Zach's mum. And then I got sent to my room to do my homework. And that's when I realised I couldn't do my homework because we had run away from school and left our bags behind.

So then I sneaked into Mum's room and phoned Zach on his new mobile phone. And that's when MISS JONES ANSWERED and she said, "IS THIS YOU, ZACH ROBERTSON?!" And I got such a fright that I slammed the phone down and dialled 999.

The police listened to everything I had to say about Miss Jones and her teddy and

the baby aliens and the Big Scissors and the ALIEN INVASION and all about the INCIDENT in the staff room with all the screaming and baby-alien teddies. And then the lady police officer on the phone told me that they would send an ALIEN UNIT to the school right away and send a police officer to my house.

Mum wasn't AT ALL happy when the police officer arrived. I tried to explain to her that he was here to see me, not her, and told her about the ALIEN UNIT. But then she just got really angry again and told me to sit on the sofa and be COMPLETELY QUIET.

So I told the
police officer
(who looked
a bit like the moon)
all about what
had happened

and he said that there had **NOT** been an
ALIEN INCIDENT at the school. And that
the **ALIEN UNIT** had checked everything
twice. And then he said that he had spoken
to the Head Teacher and that the school was
completely **ALIEN FREE**. And then he left.

Then Mum said that I should go to my
room. And she also said that under **NO**

CIRCUMSTANCES should I use the phone ever again. So I asked what would happen if she and Dad fainted simultaneously (which means at the same time) and I was not allowed to use the phone to phone an ambulance or to phone Zach. And then Mum and Dad both said, "GOODNIGHT, ISABELLA" (simultaneously).

So I just went to bed, but I couldn't sleep because I couldn't stop thinking about what the police officer that looked like the moon had said about the school being ALIEN FREE. It didn't make any sense.

It's Never Good When Your Teacher Comes to Your House

The next day, Mum said that Miss Jones had phoned and that she was bringing over my school bag, and also that she wanted to have a CHAT about everything that had happened at school yesterday.

I REALLY wasn't looking forward to Miss

Jones coming round for a CHAT (especially on a Saturday!), because usually when teachers want to have a CHAT with my mum it's because I've done something wrong.

Like the time the Head Teacher said me and Jodi couldn't sell our home-made perfume at school any more after Leanne Raynor got burns on her arms. I explained that Leanne Raynor must just have very sensitive skin and that it wasn't our fault. But then the Head Teacher said that Leanne Raynor had lost TWO LAYERS OF SKIN and then he had a CHAT with my mum and she confiscated all our perfume-making equipment.

So anyway, when Miss Jones came over, Mum told me to go up to my room. So I sat on the stairs instead, but I couldn't really hear anything except for,

"BUY ONE
GET TWO FREE",

and

"GRAVE MISTAKE".

Then when Miss Jones eventually left, Mum shouted for me to come downstairs.

So I sneaked back up and shouted, **"OK, COMING!"** and then ran down the stairs.

That's when Mum explained to me what had **REALLY** been going on at school. Mum said that because all the teachers had been working very hard this year, the Head Teacher had bought them all teddies to say thank you. But then she said about how the Head Teacher had forgotten to get teddies for the office ladies too, and that that had been a **GRAVE MISTAKE**. Mum said that the office ladies had been really angry because they had been working very hard too and didn't like being left out.

Then Mum said that the Head Teacher realised what he had done, and bought all the office ladies really cheap teddies that weren't as good as the ones he gave the teachers, and how that made everything worse! And that's why everyone was shouting in the staff room when we walked in.

Mum said they were all probably shocked to be caught arguing by pupils and that they were smiling at us so much because they were embarrassed. And then Mum said, "Poor Mr Murphy," and she giggled a bit.

So I said that that didn't really explain anything, like why Gary Petrie had tried to dance with me with his bogey fingers. And why the office ladies had said that the Head Teacher's ears must have been BURNING and that,

"THIS TEDDY SITUATION IS A TIME BOMB WAITING TO EXPLODE!"

And also that I didn't think that Mr

Killington who teaches 4K would really LIKE
a pink teddy that said, "You're Great!" on it.

And Mum said that sometimes people
say your ears are burning if someone is
gossiping about you. And that the office
ladies had been gossiping about how the
Head Teacher hadn't given THEM teddies.
Then she said that the office ladies had been
speaking METAPHORICALLY. Which
means that they didn't actually mean the
teddies were going to explode, they meant
that they were so upset about being left
out and that the SITUATION was going
to explode (which means everyone would

get angry and start shouting). And then she said that she was sure the Head Teacher had given Mr Killington a different gift. And I said I hope so. And that it should have been a bike, because I know he likes those.

Then Mum said that we should be extra nice to Miss Jones because we had given her a fright. And that it isn't OK to run out of class and worry her like that.

And then she said maybe Gary Petrie was being nice because he LIKED me! YUCK!

Something's Not Quite Right

So on Monday, we all went to see Miss Jones before class started to say sorry and to give her the five-pack of Bounty Bars Mum had made me bring (even though I told her that Cup a Soups were Miss Jones's favourite).

We told Miss Jones that we were sorry

for trying to decapitate her teddy and for running out of the classroom and for thinking that she was an alien planning an ALIEN INVASION of the school.

Miss Jones started laughing. And then she said, "Yes, your mum did mention the 'alien' thing." And then she started laughing again, and she wouldn't stop laughing for ages!

Then when she eventually stopped she said, "Why on earth would you think I was an alien?" So we told her about how it was weird when she started being nice to us all of a sudden and letting us do fun things and giving us treats and smiling and putting a

weird teddy on her desk. And she said, "Oh. I see," and then she looked a bit sad. So Jodi nudged me and I gave Miss Jones the five-pack of Bounty Bars and that made her cry a little bit, but not hysterically like before. She was crying because of happiness.

Jodi said that she must REALLY like

Bounty Bars. But I think she was so happy because we were probably the only pupils who had ever given her a gift before.

I was just about to ask if I could have one of the Bounty Bars when I realised something. There was still one thing that hadn't been explained. Why did the teddy move? The teddy hadn't been an ordinary teddy . . . it had moved! It definitely had something inside it, and I **DEFINITELY** felt it move!

So I said that we had all better go and put our coats in the lockers before class started. But I said it in my secret, **"I'M PRETENDING LIKE EVERYTHING'S FINE VOICE BUT IT'S REALLY NOT!"** And Jodi understood right away and she gave Zach a look and I started pulling Maisie out the door by her hood.

And that's when Miss Jones said, "Izzy, where IS my teddy?" And Zach started to tell her so I screamed, **"NOWHERE!"** and Jodi shouted, **"RUN!"** So we did. Again!

We rushed to the girls' toilets and all squashed into the end cubicle and Zach didn't even moan this time, he just kept saying, "What? WHAT?" And so I told them about how there was NO EXPLANATION for why the teddy had MOVED! And then Jodi said, "The whole thing's a cover!" And I explained that the teachers MUST be aliens and that we were right all along! And how they had just made up the story about the Head Teacher and the office ladies so they wouldn't get caught!

Then Jodi said we should take the teddy to the police station right away for evidence. But I said that they wouldn't believe us and that there probably wasn't any time and that we needed to decapitate the teddy, **"ONCE AND FOR ALL!"** and flush the baby aliens away.

And then someone knocked on the cubicle door and it opened because we had forgotten to lock it. And it was Miss Jones!

It's
All
Over!

We were completely trapped. I was on top of the toilet holding the teddy and Jodi and Maisie were squashed against me and Zach was trying to slide under the gap into the next toilet.

Miss Jones just stood there staring at

us. That's when I thought we were ALIEN MEAT. But then all of a sudden I felt really brave and so I said, "You're not going to get away with this, Miss Jones! We know what you REALLY are! And we know what's inside your teddy!"

That made Miss Jones's eyes go really big and then she did a little smirk. Then she pointed to the teddy and said, "Hold it tight." And so I did because I didn't want her to have it. And then she grabbed its head and ripped it off with one big pull! Then she shoved her hand into its neck hole and pulled something out. And it wasn't a bag

of baby aliens. It was a little plastic heart like the ones you get in the Teddy Factory!

Miss Jones held it out in her hand and told me to press it. So I did. And the heart started beating. And Miss Jones burst out laughing again.

But then Zach said, "What's that?" and pointed to something that was poking out of the teddy's neck ribbon. And I looked and saw a little piece of folded-up paper. And then Miss Jones pulled it out and looked at it, and then she fainted!

When Miss Jones woke up, she was pleased

that Maisie had put her in the Recovery Position, and that she wasn't hurt, but mostly she was pleased about what the piece of paper had said.

Miss Jones told us that the piece of paper was a note. And that the note had been a **MARRIAGE PROPOSAL**, and that her new boyfriend must have tucked it into the teddy's neck

WILL YOU MARRY ME?

ribbon when he gave it to her because they were IN LOVE, and that she was getting married. And we all knew that meant she was getting married to the Head Teacher because **HE** had been the one who had given her the teddy with the **PROPOSAL**. But we didn't say anything, because it was a bit disgusting and we didn't really want to think about it, even if it did explain why she had started being so nice to us. So we just said congratulations. And Zach asked if he could be the best man at the wedding and Miss Jones said she would think about it.

So everything went back to normal after that. Miss Jones wasn't an alien. There were no exploding teddies, no baby aliens and there was definitely **NO ALIEN INVASION**.

So, just like before everything happened, Miss Jones made us all sit quietly and do our work until lunch.

But then in the afternoon when we came back, the classroom didn't smell like Cup a Soup, it smelled like chocolate milk! And it didn't look **ANYTHING** like our normal classroom!

All the tables and chairs were piled up at the back and there was a **HUGE SPACESHIP**

made out of cardboard boxes in the middle of the room! And Miss Jones was dressed up like an alien!

Her face was painted green and she was wearing a long tin-foil dress! And then she

said, "WELCOME, 4J!" in a really weird voice.

"I AM TRONELLA AND TODAY WE WILL BE LEARNING ABOUT UFOS!"

Everyone ran inside and started to put on the costumes that Miss Jones had made. We couldn't believe it! Then Miss Jones smiled at me and handed me a tin-foil hat.

It was the best school day EVER! I learned loads of stuff about aliens. Like that UFO means UNIDENTIFIED FLYING OBJECT. And that some people believe that aliens landed in a place called Roswell in America in 1947.

But then Maisie turned to me and she had a weird look on her face. And I thought she was going to be sick because she'd had four alien milkshakes already. And then she said, "Miss Jones DOES seem to know an awful lot about aliens, doesn't she?"

And we all looked at Miss Jones and she

winked at us. And that's when Maisie fainted again.

Acknowledgements

I'd like to thank my fantastic agent,
Becky Bagnell, for all of her
help and for giving me a chance.

☆

Thanks also to my brilliant editor,
Kirsty Stansfield, for all of her
wise words and for finding the
crisp twin funny.

☆

Most of all, thank you to Andy, for
saying that I should. I couldn't have
done it without you.

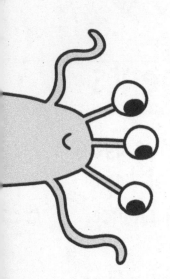

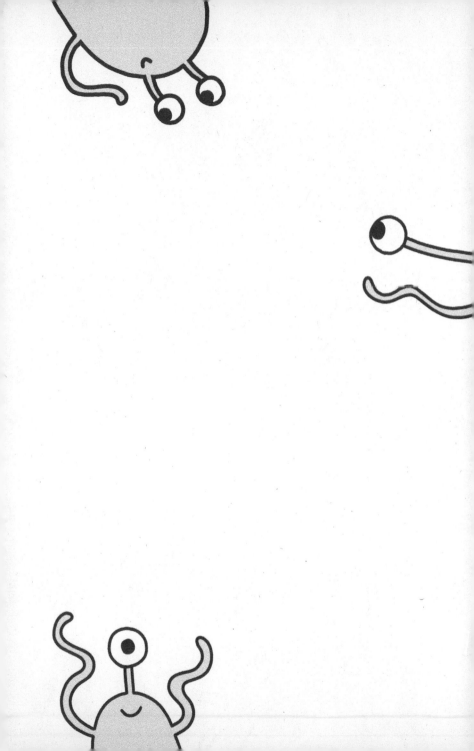